PRESS START!

ROBO-RABBIT BOY, GO!

THOMAS FLINTHAM

SCHOLASTIC

THIS ADVENTURE BELONGS TO:

....

....

START

SELECT

ROBO-RABBIT BOY, GO!

READ MORE
PRESS START!
BOOKS!

1

2

3

4

5

6

7

8

MORE BOOKS COMING SOON!

Super Rabbit Boy found the Moon Orb
at the bottom of a very deep, very dark
dungeon.

Moon Girl opens her present. An orb flies
out of the box. It floats above Animal Town.
The full moon's light shines on it.

The full moon hangs above Animal Town. Everyone is having a party. It is Moon Girl's birthday! Super Rabbit Boy has a very special present for her.

1 PRESS START!

FOR PAUL SHINN

Copyright © 2019 by Thomas Flintham

All rights reserved. Published by Scholastic Inc., *Publishers since 1920.* SCHOLASTIC, BRANCHES, and associated logos are trademarks and/or registered trademarks of Scholastic Inc.

The publisher does not have any control over and does not assume any responsibility for author or third-party websites or their content.

No part of this publication may be reproduced, stored in a retrieval system, or transmitted in any form or by any means, electronic, mechanical, photocopying, recording, or otherwise, without written permission of the publisher. For information regarding permission, write to Scholastic Inc., Attention: Permissions Department, 557 Broadway, New York, NY 10012.

This book is a work of fiction. Names, characters, places, and incidents are either the product of the author's imagination or are used fictitiously, and any resemblance to actual persons, living or dead, business establishments, events, or locales is entirely coincidental.

Library of Congress Cataloging-in-Publication Data

Names: Flintham, Thomas, author, illustrator.
Title: Robo-Rabbit Boy, go! / by Thomas Flintham.
Description: First edition. | New York : Branches/Scholastic Inc., 2019. |
Series: Press start! ; 7 | Summary: Super Rabbit Boy's present to Moon
Girl releases Queen Spooky and her army of ghosts, and Super Rabbit Boy is
taken captive—so it is up to the normally evil King Viking (who does not
like the competition of the ghost army) and especially his secret weapon,
Robo-Rabbit Boy (switched to "good" mode), to save Animal Town, release
Super Rabbit Boy, and contain the ghosts.
Identifiers: LCCN 2018055609 (print) | LCCN 2018056772 (ebook) | ISBN
9781338239836 (Ebook) | ISBN 9781338239812 (pbk. : alk. paper) | ISBN
9781338239829 (reinforced bound hardcover : alk. paper)
Subjects: LCSH: Superheroes—Juvenile fiction. | Supervillains—Juvenile
fiction. | Robots—Juvenile fiction. | Animals—Juvenile fiction. | Good
and evil—Juvenile fiction. | Video games—Juvenile fiction. | CYAC:
Superheroes—Fiction. | Supervillains—Fiction. | Robots—Fiction. |
Animals—Fiction. | Good and evil—Fiction. | Video games—Fiction.
Classification: LCC PZ7.1.F585 (ebook) | LCC PZ7.1.F585 Ro 2019 (print) | DDC
[Fic]—dc23
LC record available at https://lccn.loc.gov/2018055609

10 9 8 7 6 5 4 3 2   19 20 21 22 23

Printed in China   62
First edition, June 2019
Edited by Celia Lee
Book design by Maria Mercado

PRESS START!

ROBO-RABBIT BOY, GO!

THOMAS FLINTHAM

BRANCHES

SCHOLASTIC INC.

2 BOO

There are ghosts everywhere. Animal Town is a ghost town!

A long time ago, there was a spooky ghost troop. They haunted the world.

Finally, a true hero trapped the ghost troop inside the Moon Orb.

Only the moon's light could open the Moon Orb and free the ghosts. So the hero hid the orb in a deep, dark place.

Oh no! And then I found it!

Woooo! Thank you!

Queen Spooky grabs the Moon Orb.
There are still ghosts coming out of it.

Super Rabbit Boy is scared of ghosts! But he is a true hero. He jumps into action.

But he's caught by a ghost!

King Viking is very angry. He wants to be the only troublemaker in Animal Town!

King Viking's Robot Army charges at the ghosts.

The robots give Queen Spooky an idea.

Hmm, those robots look useful. Woo! Troop: Take over those robots!

The ghosts jump into the robots. Once inside, they take control!

BOO!

BOOOOOOOO!

Three ghost princes take control of King Viking's three powerful Robosses.

Now the ghost troop is a spooky Robo-Troop!

King Viking is really, really, really mad!

All the animals of Animal Town are scared.

King Viking has a plan.

King Viking leads the animals to a very spooky-looking castle.

Eek! It looks scary here!

Ha! <u>Wimpy</u> Rabbit Boy is afraid of ghosts. So I hid a secret in a spooky castle. He would never look here!

The animals are surprised by King Viking's secret!

Wow!

Cool!

Robo-Rabbit Boy looks just like
Super Rabbit Boy!

Oh no! Robo-Rabbit Boy is naughty!
He's not a hero!

King Viking flicks a switch. Now
Robo-Rabbit Boy is in good mode.

Robo-Rabbit Boy is ready for action. King Viking gives him a warning.

Robo-Rabbit Boy sets off. But is he a real hero? Can he save the day?

4 GHOSTS IN THE MACHINES

Robo-Rabbit Boy is excited. This is his very first adventure.

Suddenly, King Viking's robots surround Robo-Rabbit Boy. Queen Spooky's ghosts control them. They look very mean!

Robo-Rabbit Boy can hop and jump just like Super Rabbit Boy. He jumps into action. He bounces on the nearest robot.

The bounce kicks the ghost right out!

Robo-Rabbit Boy gets to work. He bounces from robot to robot.

Soon, all the robots are defeated.

Robo-Rabbit Boy runs away as fast as he can.

After a long chase, Robo-Rabbit Boy escapes.

Oh no! It's Zoombot, one of King Viking's Robosses! A ghost prince controls it. Robo-Rabbit Boy is in trouble.

Woo! I am super fast! You can't run away from me!

Oh BLIP!

Zoombot swoops toward Robo-Rabbit Boy. It wants to grab him! Robo-Rabbit Boy quickly jumps out of the way.

Zoombot speeds toward Robo-Rabbit Boy again and again. It gets closer every time.

Robo-Rabbit Boy spots a cave. He runs inside.

Zoombot swoops into the cave. It is surprised!

The cave is filled with rocks and crystals. There isn't a lot of room for a flying Zoombot.

It swoops forward! Robo-Rabbit Boy leaps behind a rock. Then another! The flying Roboss struggles to move past the rocks and crystals.

BLIP! BLIP!
You can't catch me!

Woo! I'll zoom faster!

Zoombot flies at Robo-Rabbit Boy again. This time, it goes at full speed. Robo-Rabbit Boy hops behind the nearest crystal.

Zoombot is flying too fast. It can't stop. It crashes into the crystal.

The Roboss is destroyed. Robot pieces lie all over the floor. The ghost prince isn't there. Where has he gone?

The ghost prince's voice echoes from a crystal.

Suddenly, Robo-Rabbit Boy's ears start to ring. It's King Viking.

Robo-Rabbit Boy can now fly with the gold part! He flies out of the cave.

Robo-Rabbit Boy zooms straight toward Mount Moon. But something pulls him back.

Oh no! It's Vacubot, another Roboss!
Vacubot has a special funnel. It can vaccum
anything. It pulls in Robo-Rabbit Boy!

Boo! You can't fly
away from me.

45

Robo-Rabbit Boy tries to fly away as hard as he can. But he can't beat Vacubot.

Robo-Rabbit Boy has an idea. He takes the crystal and throws it at Vacubot.

The Vacubot quickly sucks up the crystal and starts to shake.

The Roboss implodes! And the crystal traps the second ghost prince!

OUTSMARTED

Robo-Rabbit Boy searches the robot pieces.
He spots Vacubot's special gold robot part.
It's the vacuum!

Robo-Rabbit Boy turns around. It's a robot.
It looks very weak.

You have beaten
two Robosses. And
you trapped my two
ghost brothers!

You must be the third
ghost prince! Get out
of that Roboss!

Robo-Rabbit Boy springs into action! He flies at the Roboss as fast as he can. The robot easily dodges him.

Robo-Rabbit Boy tries to use his vacuum. The robot ducks behind a big rock before the vacuum gets to it.

Robo-Rabbit Boy is surprised. The Roboss looks weak, but Robo-Rabbit Boy's powers don't work on it.

Smartbot knows every move Robo-Rabbit Boy plans to make!

Robo-Rabbit Boy is in trouble. The Smartbot is ready for his plans. Then he has an idea!

Robo-Rabbit Boy closes his eyes and starts to fly. He zooms and swoops around. He turns his vacuum on.

Robo-Rabbit Boy flies faster and faster.
He heads straight for a sharp rock. Oh no!

Will this new nonthinking plan work?

Just in time, Robo-Rabbit Boy springs off the rock! He bounces all over the place. Backward and forward. Up and down. Loop-the-loop.

He doesn't think. He doesn't see. Smartbot is mad. It doesn't know what Robo-Rabbit Boy is doing!

Finally, Robo-Rabbit Boy zooms toward Smartbot. The Roboss doesn't know what to do. It is confused!

Waaaaa! What are you thinking?

Nothing!

Suddenly, Robo-Rabbit Boy bumps the crystal into Smartbot. The Roboss breaks apart. The crystal traps the final ghost prince.

He clicks Smartbot's Super Brain Computer Chip into his head. Now he has all three Robosses' special robot parts!

Robo-Rabbit Boy looks at the Roboss parts around him. Robo-Rabbit Boy is faster, more powerful, and smarter now. But can he defeat Queen Spooky?

Suddenly, his Super Brain Computer Chip gives him a super idea.

I can use these robot parts to make a robot hero upgrade!

Robo-Rabbit Boy 2.0 is done! He zooms toward Mount Moon. The ghosts are waiting.

Robo-Rabbit Boy turns on his 2.0 ghost trap! The vacuum pulls in all the ghosts. They can't get away. The crystal locks them all in.

Woooo! Boooo!

Let us out!

Boooo! Wooo!

Now the mountain is ghost free. Robo-Rabbit Boy zooms toward the top.

Here I come, Queen Spooky!

Queen Spooky waits at the top of the mountain. Poor Super Rabbit Boy is tied up. The Moon Orb has stopped glowing. Finally, all the ghosts have come out of it.

Who are you?

I'm **Robo-Rabbit Boy. King Viking** built me to save the day!

Robo-Rabbit Boy turns on the ghost trap again. It's so powerful! Queen Spooky and her ghosts can't get away.

Robo-Rabbit Boy did it! He caught all the ghosts and saved Super Rabbit Boy.

The ghosts in the crystal sound very unhappy!

Just then, Robo-Rabbit Boy's chest starts to beep.

What is that noise?

It's something I made. You see, King Viking built me to have all your powers.

But he forgot one thing. A true hero power. So I built it.

What did you build?

68

SCARY FUN!

Robo-Rabbit Boy takes Super Rabbit Boy back to the scary castle.

Inside, Robo-Rabbit Boy shares his plan.
The ghosts can all live with him here!

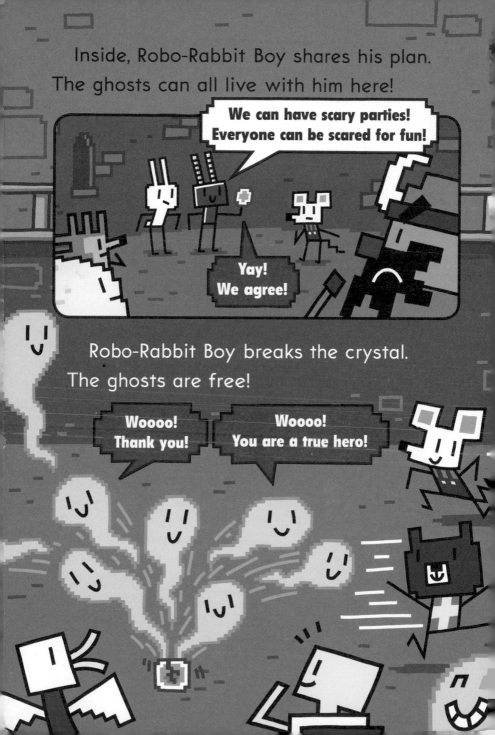

We can have scary parties! Everyone can be scared for fun!

Yay! We agree!

Robo-Rabbit Boy breaks the crystal.
The ghosts are free!

Woooo! Thank you!

Woooo! You are a true hero!

It's a spooky party! All of Animal Town joins the fun.

72

THOMAS FLINTHAM

has always loved to draw and tell stories, and now that is his job! He grew up in Lincoln, England, and studied illustration in Camberwell, London. He lives by the sea with his wife, Bethany, in Cornwall.

Thomas is the creator of THOMAS FLINTHAM'S BOOK OF MAZES AND PUZZLES and many other books for kids. PRESS START! is his first early chapter book series.

Who is giving Super Rabbit Boy a scare? Connect the dots to find out!

PRESS START!

How much do you know about
ROBO-RABBIT BOY, GO!?

Why is Moon Girl afraid of the Moon Orb?

Look at the picture on page 4. What kind of creatures do you see hiding in the dungeon?

What are the three gold robot parts Robo-Rabbit Boy finds?

How does Robo-Rabbit Boy become a true hero?

Robo-Rabbit Boy lives in a spooky castle with many ghost friends. Use words and pictures to describe what kind of castle you would like to live in.

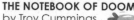

IT'S ALWAYS GAME ON WITH SUPER RABBIT BOY!

Uh-oh, Super Rabbit Boy is in big trouble. Queen Spooky and her ghost troop have captured him! It's up to Robo-Rabbit Boy to help. Robo-Rabbit Boy is fast like Super Rabbit Boy and strong like Super Rabbit Boy. But can a robot really be a true hero? This latest Press Start! adventure is fully **CHARGED**!

Select your next **PRESS START!** adventure!

PRESS START!

SUPER RABBIT ALL-STARS!

SCHOLASTIC
scholastic.com/branches

APPEALS TO
1ST-2ND GRADERS

READING LEVEL
GRADE 2

Find more leveling information for this book at:
scholastic.com/brancheslevels

Cover art by Thomas Flintham
Cover design by Maria Mercado

$4.99 US / $6.99 CAN

ISBN 978-1-338-23981-2
50499

9 781338 239812

W8-AST-513